About The Book

In a future where technology has redefined the boundaries of life itself, Nanonaut takes readers on an unforgettable journey into the uncharted realms of science, survival, and the human spirit.

When innovation collides with morality, and microscopic machines hold the power to alter existence, one decision can reshape the fate of humanity. Blending cutting-edge science fiction with deep questions about identity, resilience, and sacrifice, Nanonaut challenges what it truly means to be human.

Perfect for fans of visionary science fiction and thought-provoking storytelling, Nanonaut delivers a gripping adventure that lingers long after the last page.

Wayne Stewart is a passionate storyteller who blends science, imagination, and human emotions to craft compelling narratives. With a deep interest in futuristic technology and its impact on society, Wayne brings fresh perspectives to modern science fiction, grounded in plausible reality. Nanonaut reflects his firm belief that even in the face of rapid innovation, the human element remains at the core of every story.

www.ingramcontent.com/pod-product-compliance
Lightning Source LLC
Chambersburg PA
CBHW041147250626
47164CB00013B/13